W9-BAN-914

Fairy Tales with a Twist

PICTURE WINDOW BOOKS
a capstone imprint

Another
Other Side
of the
Story

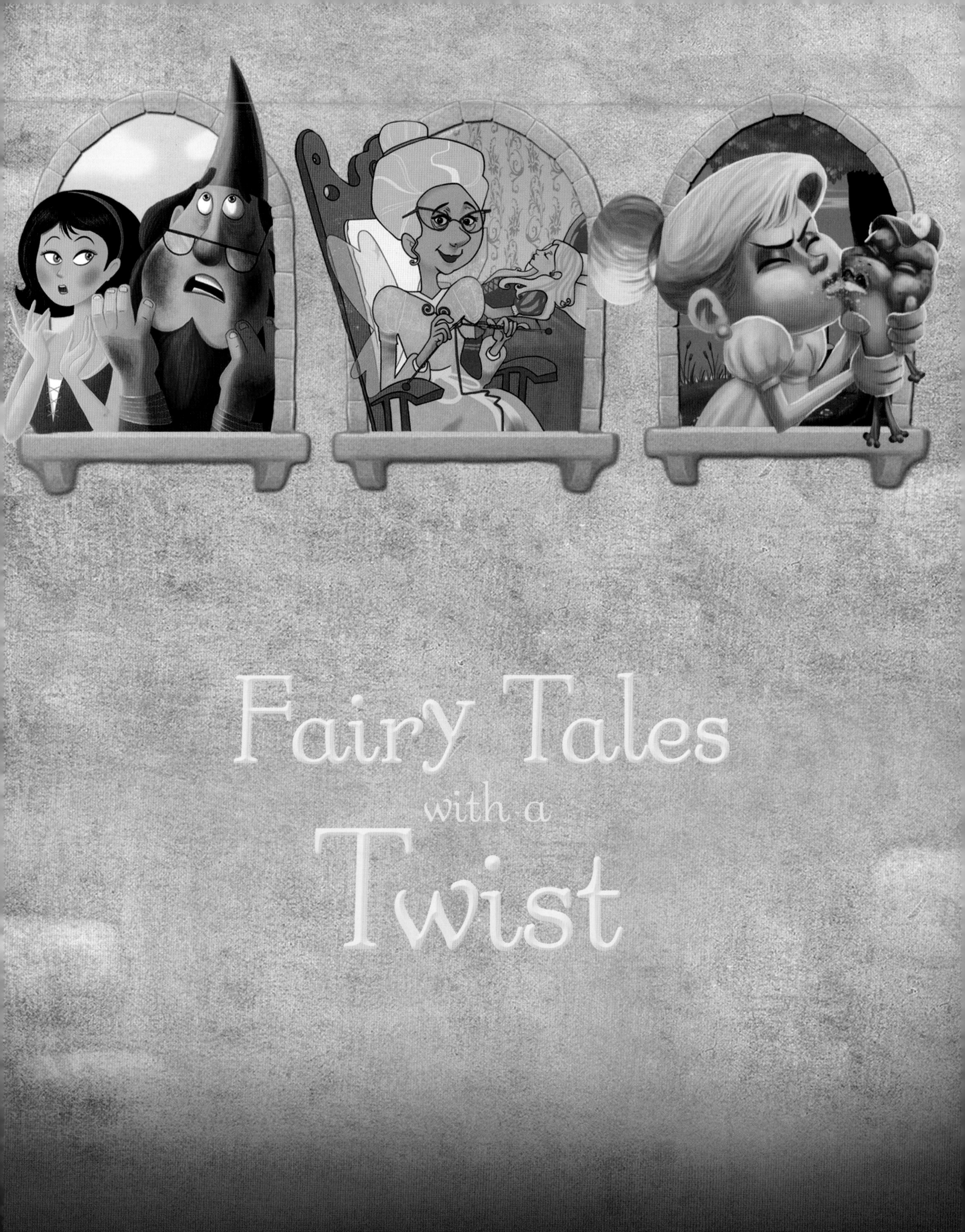
Fairy Tales
with a
Twist

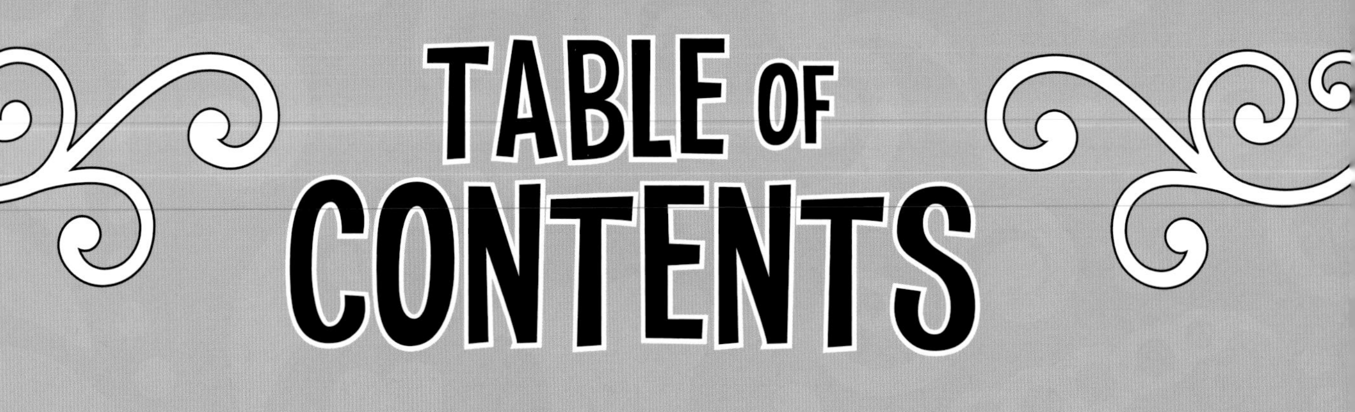

TABLE OF CONTENTS

No Lie, I Acted Like a Beast!
THE STORY OF BEAUTY AND THE BEAST
as Told by the Beast

Page 6

Seriously, Snow White Was SO Forgetful!
THE STORY OF SNOW WHITE
as Told by the Dwarves

Page 28

Really, Rapunzel Needed a Haircut!
THE STORY OF
RAPUNZEL
as Told by Dame Gothel
Page 50

Truly, We Both Loved Beauty Dearly!
THE STORY OF
SLEEPING BEAUTY
as Told by the Good and Bad Fairies
Page 72

Frankly, I Never Wanted to Kiss Anybody!
THE STORY OF
THE FROG PRINCE
as Told by the Frog
Page 94

NO LIE, I ACTED LIKE A BEAST!

The Story of BEAUTY AND THE BEAST as Told by THE BEAST

by **Nancy Loewen**
illustrated by **Cristian Bernardini**

Yup, I've still got it.

I might not look like a beast anymore, but I can still act the part. Notice that I used the word "act"? Acting changed my life. It got me INTO trouble. It got me OUT of trouble. It even got me the girl of my dreams!

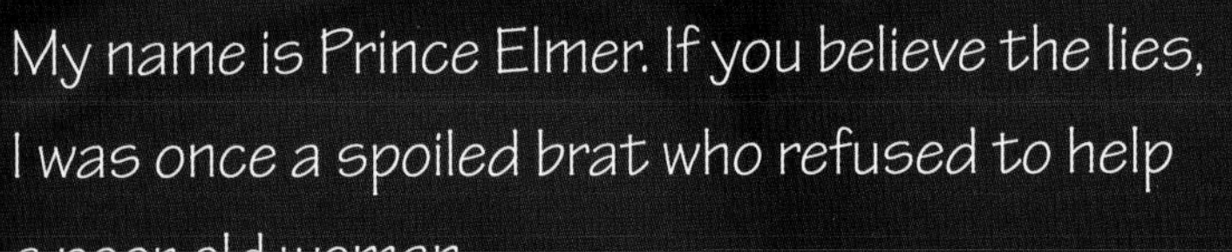

My name is Prince Elmer. If you believe the lies,
I was once a spoiled brat who refused to help
a poor old woman.

Here's the REAL story.

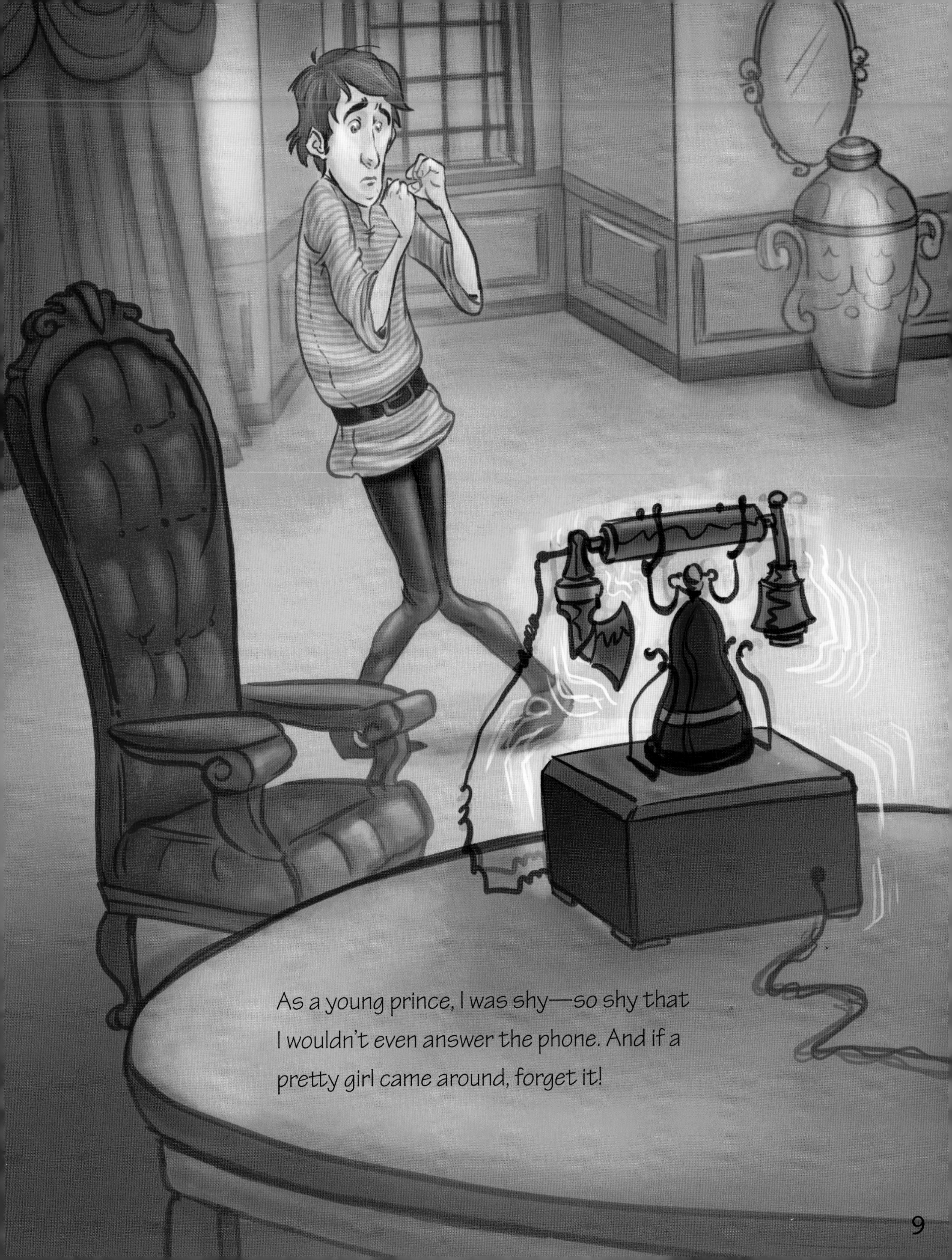

As a young prince, I was shy—so shy that I wouldn't *even* answer the phone. And if a pretty *girl* came around, forget it!

One day I read a notice in the newspaper.

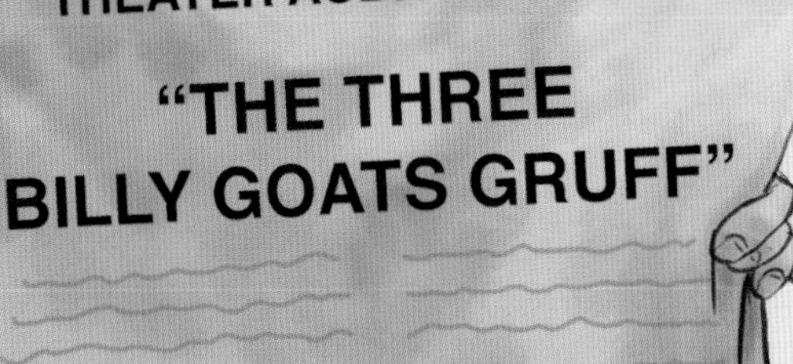

I decided then and there that I was done being shy. I was going to find my voice—as an actor!

Of course I wanted the best part in the play: the evil troll who lives under the bridge. So I practiced. And practiced.

I barked and hissed.

I growled as I
brushed my teeth.

I slashed at
the air with
my fork.

On audition night, my head was so full of troll thoughts that at first I didn't notice the tug on my sleeve. It was a poor old woman asking for food.

"NO!" I roared. "I WON'T HELP YOU. GO AWAY!"

Then I remembered that I wasn't actually a troll. "Oh! I'm so sorry, I was just—"

But it was too late. Before my eyes, the old woman became an evil fairy. "Fool!" she cried. "You act like a beast. You shall BE a beast!"

"But you don't understand—"

"There is only one way to break this spell," the evil fairy said. "A woman must fall in love with you, in spite of your looks!" She snickered. "Like that's going to happen."

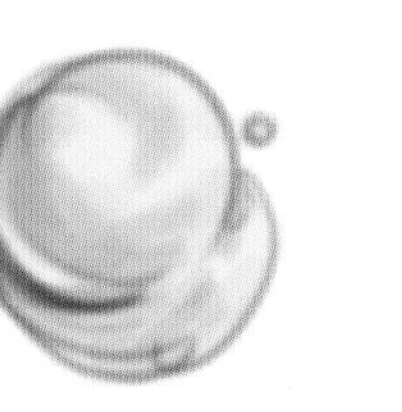

I must've fainted, because the next thing I knew, I was in a strange castle. In the woods. Alone.

That was the worst time of my life. I was hideous. Oh, sure, I had all sorts of fine things. But I had no one to talk to.

To pass the time, I kept up my acting studies. In the garden
I put on one-man shows for the birds and the butterflies.

Then came the stormy night that changed everything. A lost traveler took shelter in my castle. I remained hidden, but I made sure he had everything he needed. It felt awfully nice to have company.

The next morning, as he was leaving, he took a rose from the garden. That gave me an idea. Maybe I could trick him into coming back.

I'm not proud of what I did next, but it worked!

"IS THAT HOW YOU REWARD MY KINDNESS?" I roared. **"YOU WILL PAY WITH YOUR LIFE!"**

The man *begged* to say good-bye to his family. He promised to return.

And he *did*—with his daughter named Beauty. Beauty had vowed to take her father's place. She felt responsible because she was the one who'd asked for a rose.

For me, it was love at first sight. For her—not so much. Who could blame her? I had fur growing out of my nostrils. And I smelled like a barn.

I went back to my shy ways, hiding behind drapes and ducking into closets. After a few days passed, Beauty figured out that I was more of a teddy bear than a beast. Imagine my delight when SHE started talking to ME.

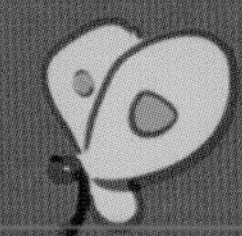

We had a lot in common—including a love of *good* theater. I didn't have to do one-man shows anymore. I had a co-star! The more Beauty and I acted together, the more she got to know the real me.

One day, Beauty asked to leave the castle.
She wanted to visit her family.

"OK, but you'd better come back. I'll die without you," I joked. And then my voice became serious. "Really. If you leave me, I'll die."

Yes, it was a bit over the top. What can I say? I'm an actor.

And with that,
she left.

When Beauty returned, she found me lying on the ground next to the rose bush. I tried not to breathe.

"Beast?" Beauty cried out. "Oh, no!"

Her tears poured onto my fur, but I didn't move.

"Oh, Beast, you're the ugliest creature I've ever seen. But—I can't help it, I love you! I do!"

And just like that, the spell was broken.
I got my Happily Ever After.

I was a prince again.

I married Beauty.

And together we've opened the Prince Elmer School of Beastly Good Acting.

You should take a class. It might change your life!

THE END

NEXT UP ... The Story of Snow White

OF COURSE YOU THINK SNOW WHITE WAS THE MOST PERFECT GIRL IN THE WORLD. WHY, JUST LOOK AT HER! BUT THERE'S MORE TO THE STORY. AND THE DWARVES BEHIND THIS PAGE ARE READY TO GIVE YOU AN EARFUL ...

Seriously, SNOW WHITE WAS *SO* FORGETFUL!

The Story of SNOW WHITE as Told by THE DWARVES

by Nancy Loewen illustrated by Gerald Guerlais

I love Snow White *dearly*. She's a beautiful person, inside and out.

But honestly, the girl's got a mind like a leaky bucket.

Here's the REAL story of Snow White and the Seven Dwarves. (My name, by the way, is Seven. We dwarves *used* to have real names, but Snow White couldn't remember them.)

One day, we came home from the mines to find our cottage door open. We thought we'd been burgled! But no. It was just a lovely little girl, sound asleep.

In the morning she had quite a story to tell.

“Hello!” she said. “I’m Snow White. The queen sent me into the woods, and a hunter was supposed to kill me, but he was nice and let me go, and I wandered a long time in the woods. I guess I’m very pretty, and that’s why the queen doesn’t like me. I’m Snow White. Would it be all right if I lived with you? I love playing house, and keeping house for real wouldn’t be all that different, would it? Did I tell you my name is Snow White?”

Wow, did she have energy.

Life with Snow White was ... interesting. She'd forget to turn on the stove. She'd forget to turn it *off*.

She'd make banana cream pie and forget the bananas.

She'd knit scarves that were 10 feet long—just *because* she forgot to stop.

On the bright side, she laughed at all of our jokes. And she never complained about anything.

Years passed. Snow White grew up, but she didn't really change. She remained her sweet, charming, forgetful self.

Then one day, Five heard a rumor.

"The queen knows Snow White is alive!" he told us.
"The magic mirror spilled the beans!"

We gave Snow White orders to stay inside the cottage. She was not to open the door to anyone. We knew the evil queen would try to hurt her.

But Snow White quickly forgot. Twice we came home to find her lying on the floor. It was clearly the work of the queen.

The first time, Snow White couldn't breathe. She was wearing a brand-new corset that was laced too tightly.

The second time she had a poisoned comb in her hair.

All the queen had to do was dress up as an old woman and offer something pretty for sale. Any thoughts of being careful went right out of Snow White's head!

We posted reminders. We *even* wrote

DO NOT OPEN THE DOOR

in syrup on her pancakes.

But once again we came home to find Snow White on the floor. This time we couldn't help her. There was no corset to loosen or comb to remove. We thought she was dead, killed by a magical spell. And yet, days passed, and she remained as lovely as ever.

"It's like she's forgotten how to wake up," Five whispered.

We couldn't make ourselves bury her. So we placed Snow White in a glass coffin and brought her to a spot on the mountainside. We took turns guarding her.

Thank goodness, that's not the end of the story!

One day I heard voices
in the woods.

No, your majesty, it's not time for lunch. We ate our lunch an hour ago. Don't you remember?

Oh, right! Silly me.

Suddenly I was face-to-face with a prince! But he barely noticed me. He couldn't take his eyes off Snow White.

"What happened to her?" he asked. "What's her name?"

I told him the whole story.

"She's the most beautiful girl I've ever seen," he breathed. "Those lips, those eyes! What did you say her name was? Could I take her with me? Now that I've seen her, I don't think I can live without her! What silky hair she has! Tell me again, what's her name?"

I smiled. The prince reminded me of a certain someone.

We were bringing Snow White back to the cottage, so the other dwarves could say good-bye. Without warning the prince stopped and turned around. "Hey, what about lunch?" he asked.

The servants slipped.
The coffin slid.
And Snow White coughed.

I'd never heard such a beautiful sound. Out of her throat flew a bit of rosy red apple. Rosy red POISONED apple, that is.

She sat up. **"Did someone say something about lunch?"** she asked.

Yes, Snow White married the prince, of course.

The *queen* actually showed up at the reception, if you can believe it. Everyone threw dinner rolls at her and booed so loudly that she ran away and was never heard from again.

Things are pretty much back to normal now. When it gets cold outside, we're grateful for our 10-foot scarves. And every once in a while, we make banana cream pie without any bananas. Just for old times' sake.

THE END

NEXT UP ... The Story of Rapunzel

OF COURSE YOU THINK

DAME GOTHEL WAS A HORRIBLE OLD WITCH, LOCKING LONG-HAIRED RAPUNZEL IN THAT TALL, TALL TOWER. YOU DON'T KNOW HER SIDE OF THE STORY. WELL, SHE'S STANDING RIGHT BEHIND THIS PAGE, AND SHE'S EAGER TO TALK ...

REALLY, RAPUNZEL NEEDED A HAIRCUT!

The Story of RAPUNZEL as Told by DAME GOTHEL

by
Jessica Gunderson

illustrated by
Denis Alonso

Let me tell you, it's lonely being a witch. When folks find out what I am, they steer clear. I have no friends at all. Not one. It's unfair, really.

A sweet girl with beautiful hair once lived with me. And I used to have a fantastic garden. (Neither the girl nor the plants cared one whit that I was a witch.) My flowers bloomed bright and tall. My radishes were to die for. But, sadly, I haven't seen the girl or my garden in a while. It all started when a neighbor tried to *steal* my radishes ...

Here's how it went:

"My wife is going to have a baby," my neighbor stammered. "And she craves your radishes. She swears if she doesn't get them, she'll just die!"

"OK," I said. "But what will you *give* me in return? I can *get* a pretty penny for these at the Farmers' Market, you know."

"But I have no money. Not a single *dime*!" he whined. "Maybe I'll *give* you our baby? We can always have more, I *guess*."

Of *course* I *agreed*. A *baby* would be *better* than *gold*! It would *cure* my loneliness!

When the time came, the man brought baby Rapunzel to me. I raised Rapunzel as my own daughter and gave her anything she wanted from my garden: turnips, potatoes, berries, cucumbers ... But do you know what her favorite food was?

Radishes.

The girl had good taste.

All those vegetables helped Rapunzel's hair grow long and red. She sang sweet songs as she helped me tend the garden.

The longer Rapunzel's hair grew, the more she loved it. She washed it and combed it and brushed it and braided it. And then she washed it again. You have no idea how much I spent on shampoo.

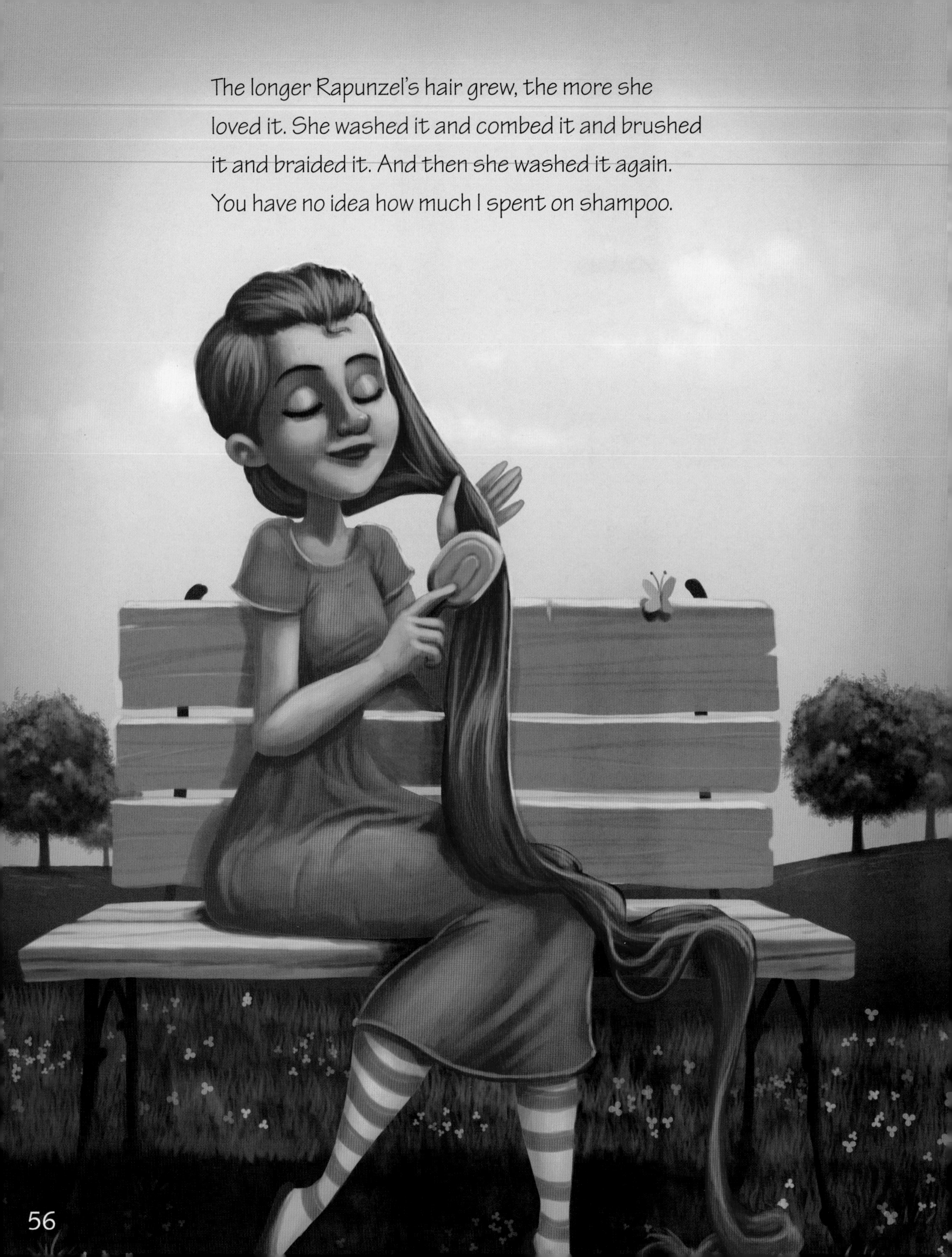

One day a group of neighbors gathered outside my garden. I heard them whispering. Plotting. Planning. This time, however, no one wanted to steal my radishes. Nope. They wanted to steal *Rapunzel* and use her hair for wigs!

So I did what any mother would do.
I locked the girl away in a tower.

"Rapunzel, let down your hair!"

I would call. And she would lean out of the window and wrap her hair around a hook. Then I'd climb up.

Every day without fail, I brought her vegetables from the garden. At first she seemed content. But one day she told me she was lonely. And if anyone knows how loneliness feels, it's me. "How can I help?" I asked.

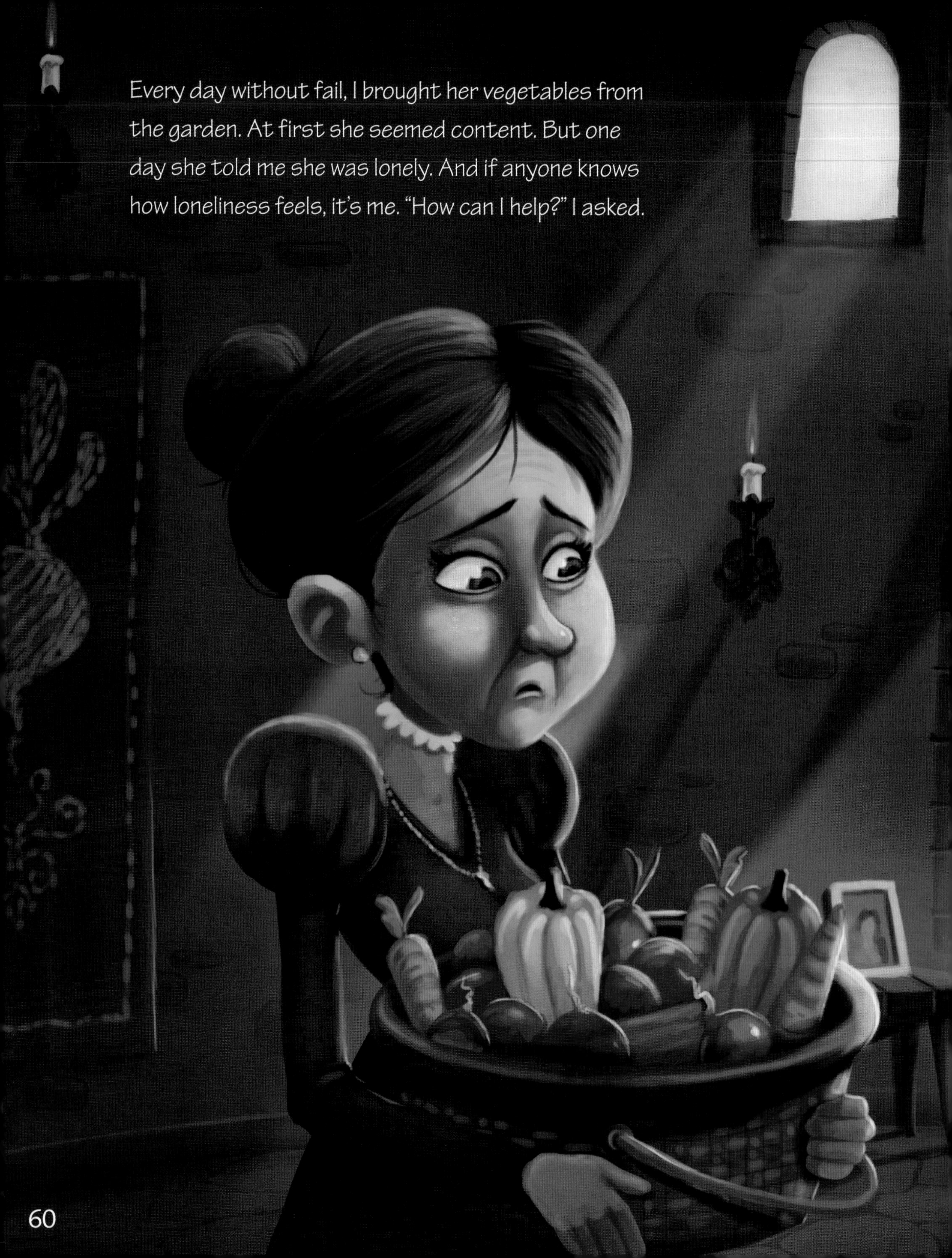

"Bring me every mirror you can find," Rapunzel said.

"Then I can keep myself company."

Hauling a load of mirrors to the tower wasn't my idea of fun, but I did it anyway. I spent a week gathering every mirror in the village. Then I lugged them, one by one, into the tower. Let me tell you, it was not an easy task for an old witch like me.

"Thanks!" Rapunzel said. "But I don't need
the mirrors anymore. I met a handsome
prince. He climbs up to visit me every day."

"What?" I roared, my voice rattling the windows and shattering the mirrors.

"He's going to steal you away!"

I panicked. What could I do? How could I keep the prince away? In a blink I grabbed Rapunzel's hair and chopped it off. Clumps of it.

Rapunzel wailed. I admit I felt a little bad. "It'll grow back," I comforted.

"Short hair will be nice for the summer. Cooler."

But she would not stop crying.

"Let's go home, dear," I said. "I'll make you a radish salad, OK?" I fastened her hair clippings to the hook, and we crawled down together.

While Rapunzel chomped her salad, I returned to the tower and waited.

"Rapunzel! Let down your hair!" the prince called.

I lowered Rapunzel's hair, and the prince climbed up.

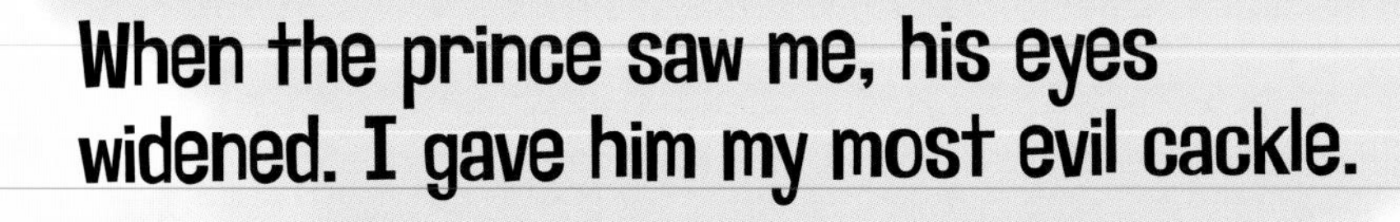

When the prince saw me, his eyes widened. I gave him my most evil cackle.

I'd meant only to *scare* him a little, *but he leaped* out of the window and *landed* on some thorny bushes below. The *poor boy staggered* about, *clutching* his *eyes*. I was *going* to climb down and help him, but he *did* a *terrible* thing. He reached for Rapunzel's hair and yanked it from the hook. Then he ran away.

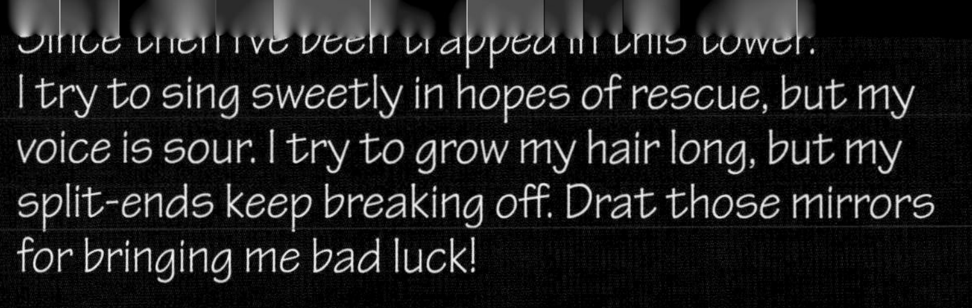

Since then I've been trapped in this tower.
I try to sing sweetly in hopes of rescue, but my voice is sour. I try to grow my hair long, but my split-ends keep breaking off. Drat those mirrors for bringing me bad luck!

A little bird told me Rapunzel and her prince got married. I'm sorry I missed the wedding. It sounded lovely. Do you know what the bride carried? A bouquet of radish roses!

THE END

NEXT UP ... The Story of Sleeping Beauty

OF COURSE YOU THINK THE FAIRIES WERE EVIL AND SPITEFUL, CURSING SLEEPING BEAUTY WITH A FOREVER SLEEP. UNTIL NOW, YOU'VE HEARD ONLY ONE SIDE OF THE STORY. TURN THE PAGE, AND HEAR WHAT THE FAIRIES HAVE TO SAY ...

TRULY, WE BOTH LOVED BEAUTY DEARLY!

The Story of SLEEPING BEAUTY as Told by THE GOOD AND BAD FAIRIES

by **Trisha Speed Shaskan**

illustrated by **Amit Tayal**

People around here call me the Bad Fairy, or "BF." My real name is Edna. I'm the one who cast that spell on *Sleeping Beauty*. That's not the whole story, though. The story begins before Beauty was born, when BF used to mean something different.

I'm Edna's younger sister. I'm the so-called Good Fairy, otherwise known as Stella. You can't count on my sister for the whole story. I'm the one who knows it all.

Pish posh, Stella! I'm more than 500 years old. I'M the one who knows it all. Now let me tell the story, please. I first met the king long ago. We became friends, and he named me his BF (which stood for "Best Fairy" back then). I bewitched his castle. It still sparkles to this day.

Yes, Edna was once the king's BF. But over time, her mind got a little rusty. During one Lunar Festival, Edna overdid it and made the moon glow too brightly. It nearly blinded everyone. I told her to stop.

"Moonlight," Edna said, **"time to drop!"**
(She was supposed to say, **"Time to STOP!"**)

The moon dropped. Fast!

After that, Edna wasn't invited to anything. It was just too dangerous to have her around.

One day the king and queen announced the biggest party ever: a feast for their new baby girl, the princess. All the fairies, except Edna, were invited. Each of us prepared a special gift. I worked on Gracefulness (because, you know, a princess shouldn't be klutzy).

I did NOT *get* invited to the feast. A mistake, surely. The king wouldn't forget his BF, would he? So I prepared my *gift* for the princess: Compassion. Every princess needs the *ability* to feel and understand the troubles of her people, right?

On the day of the feast, the guard checked the guest list. I wasn't on it.

I had never felt so bad in all my life.

I loved the princess dearly, and I was going to give her my gift—with or without an invitation.

So I fired up my wings and flew in through a window. Stella was just about to give her gift of Gracefulness.

"On the princess' 16th birthday," I shouted, "she will prick her finger on a magic spinning wheel! The wound will stand for the suffering of the people of her kingdom! And it will remind the princess to be kind!"

Edna's spell began well enough. But then she said, "Don't worry, dear princess. When you die, your tears will comfort lives!"

(She was supposed to say, "When you CRY!")

I don't have Edna's ancient powers. But I did my best to fix the mess. My NEW gift to the princess was that she WOULDN'T die on her 16th birthday. Instead, she would prick her finger and fall asleep for 100 years.

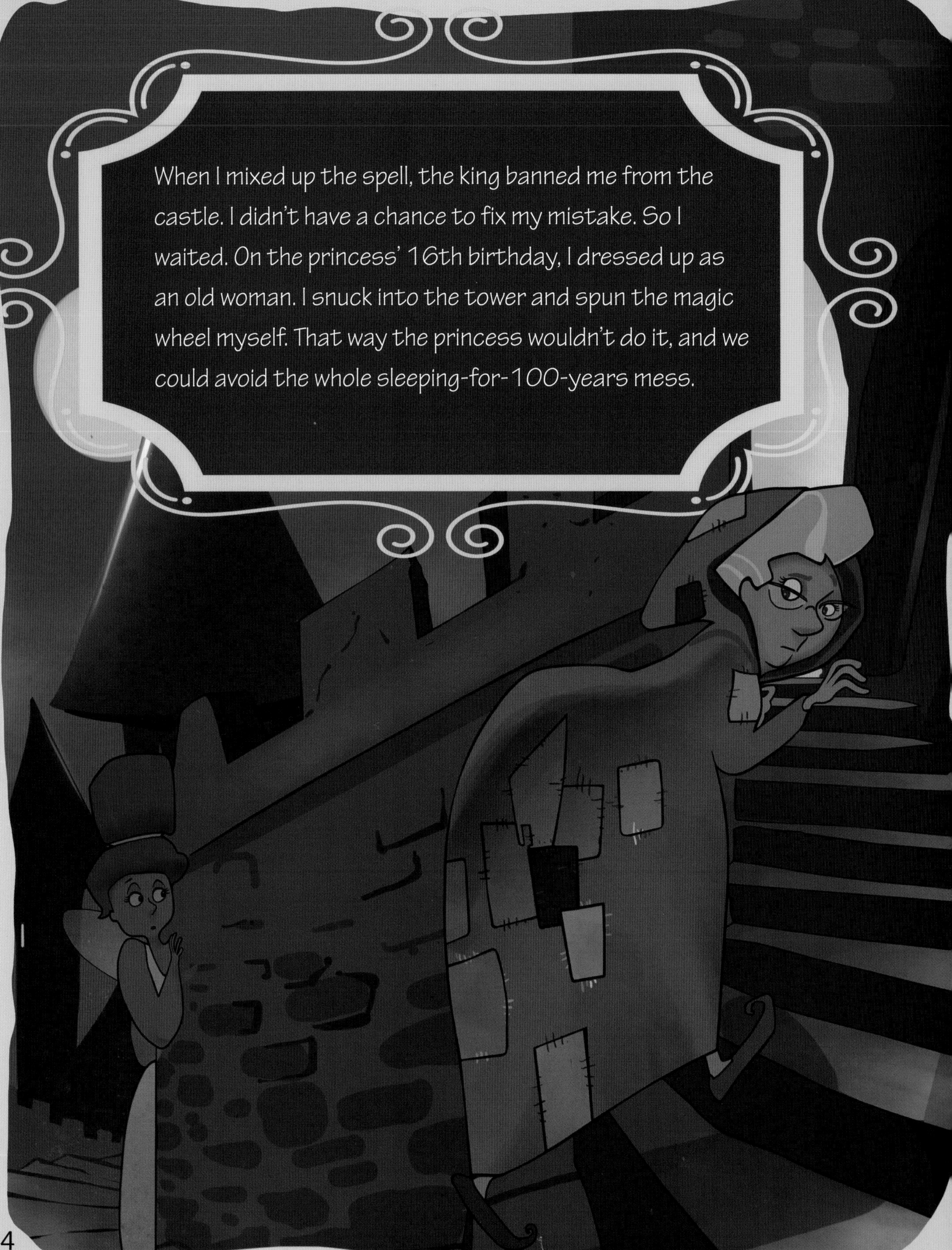

When I mixed up the spell, the king banned me from the castle. I didn't have a chance to fix my mistake. So I waited. On the princess' 16th birthday, I dressed up as an old woman. I snuck into the tower and spun the magic wheel myself. That way the princess wouldn't do it, and we could avoid the whole sleeping-for-100-years mess.

I knew Edna was up to something, so I followed her. Her plan began OK. But then the princess walked in. She'd seen a light in the tower.

"Go away!" Edna yelled.

But it was too late. The princess had already stumbled and pricked her finger. What a klutz.

I did the only thing I could do: I put the entire castle to sleep. Vines grew and spread. They covered the walls and the tower where the princess slept.

For years everyone snoozed. Over time, word traveled of the lovely "Sleeping Beauty." (Fairies checked in on her, you know.) Many princes tried to climb the tower. None had any luck.

I felt dreadful and stayed far, far away. I didn't want to make things worse. But how much worse could they get?

Finally I decided I HAD to make things right. I dressed up as an old woman again and returned to the castle. A prince entered the castle grounds. I waved my wand and chanted:

**"Compassion is the fullest of gifts.
Compassion will bless you and your lips."**

The vines fell off the tower. The prince ran up the stairs.

Stella (who was spying on me again) flew up with me just in time to see the prince kiss the princess. At that moment, the castle sparkled. Everyone woke.

No one, except my sister, ever knew I was the one who broke the spell. People still call me the Bad Fairy. But that's OK. I was happy to hear the prince and princess had a lovely wedding. And I'm already working on a gift for THEIR new baby girl!
THE END

AND FINALLY ... The Story of the Frog Prince

OF COURSE YOU THINK THE FROG NEEDED A KISS FROM A BEAUTIFUL PRINCESS TO END HIS "TOADALLY" AWFUL CURSE. YOU DON'T KNOW THE OTHER SIDE OF THE STORY. WELL, FLIP THE PAGE, AND LET THE FROG TELL YOU HIMSELF ...

Frankly, I NEVER WANTED TO KISS ANYBODY!

The Story of THE FROG PRINCE as Told by THE FROG

by Nancy Loewen

illustrated by Denis Alonso

"You have to kiss a lot of frogs to find your prince."

I bet you've heard that one before. And I bet you're thinking—

EEEWWWWW!

Kissing a frog would be gross!

Well, I just happen to be the former frog who inspired that saying. My name is Prince Puckett. And let me tell you, that kiss was no picnic for me either! Here's the REAL story.

THE FROG PRINCE

I was playing baseball the day Hank's mom turned me into a frog. One moment I was about to catch Hank's pop fly—which would give my team the championship—

and the next moment I was flopping around on the ground with more legs than I knew what to do with.

"Sorry, kid," Hank's mom called as she was led out of the ballpark. "To break the spell, just get a princess to kiss you. But she can't know you're a prince!"

Well, whether I was a prince or a frog, I wasn't about to kiss any girl. And I soon found that being a frog had its perks.

I could see almost all the way around my head.

I could swim and dive like nobody's business.

And boy, could I jump!

I jumped and jumped all the way to a new home, near a well under an old linden tree.

One day I was playing kick-the-mushroom with my frog buddies when I heard the unmistakable sound of a ball smacking into a glove.

"That's the princess," Mickey told me. "She's always coming out here to practice."

I listened to the **smack ... smack ... smack.**
And I wished that I could be just a regular
baseball-playing prince again.

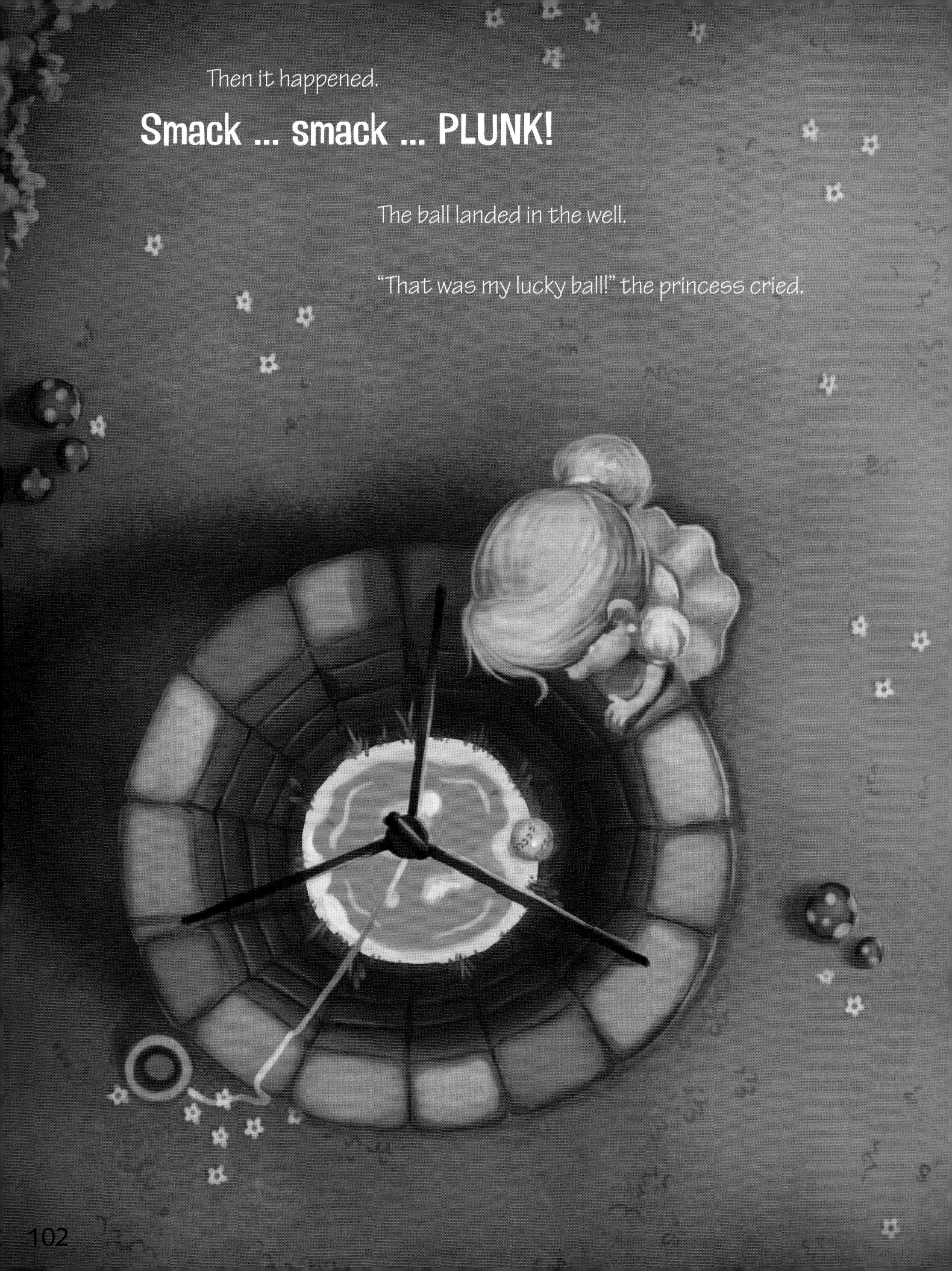

Then it happened.

Smack ... smack ... PLUNK!

The ball landed in the well.

"That was my lucky ball!" the princess cried.

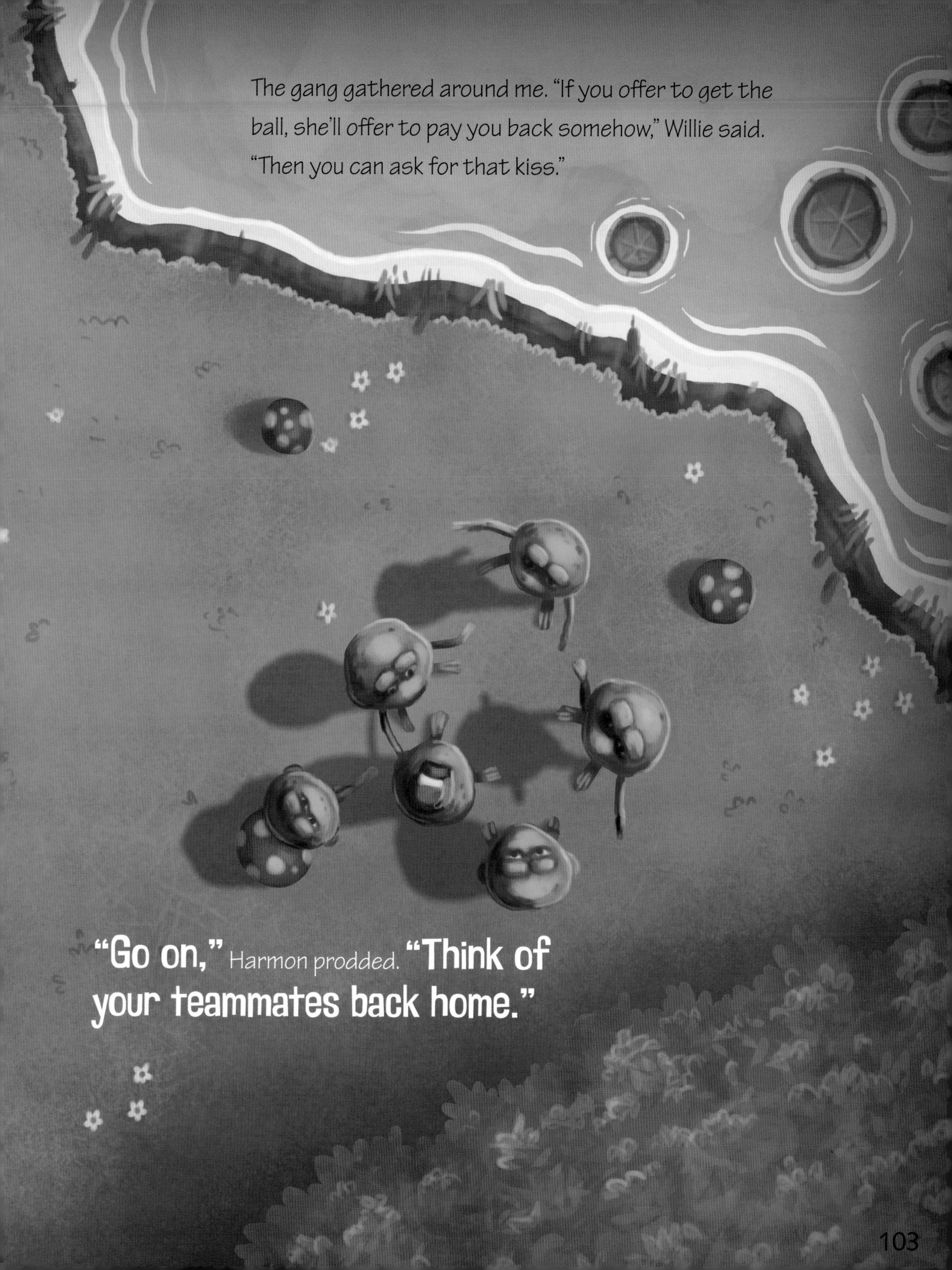

The *gang gathered* around me. "If you offer to *get* the ball, she'll offer to pay you back somehow," Willie said. "Then you can ask for that kiss."

"Go on," *Harmon prodded.* **"Think of your teammates back home."**

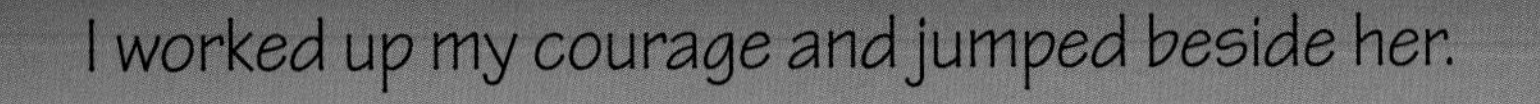

I worked up my courage and jumped beside her.

"Would you like me to get your ball?" I asked.

"You?" she asked. "Well, I guess it wouldn't hurt to try."

I hopped into the well and kicked the ball out.

"How can I *ever* repay you?" the princess asked. "Just ask and it's yours!"

"You can ... I mean ... I'd like a ...," I stammered. Finally I blurted out,

"A kiss! I want you to kiss me!"

"Bleh!" the princess said.

We stared at each other.

She leaned toward me.

I leaned toward her.

“Nope, can’t do it!” she said.

She took her ball and ran away.

Well, that made me a little mad. A deal's a deal, right?

It took me awhile, but jump by jump I followed her back to her castle.

The princess wouldn't open the door, but I stood there croaking loudly until her father, the king himself, let me in. I told him about our agreement.

**"My daughter must keep her word,"
the king assured me in a booming voice.**

Then he plopped me down on the dinner table, right next to her.

The princess looked the other way. "I'll kiss you after we eat," she said. "Promise."

But as soon as she'd swallowed her last bite of lemon tart, she dashed up the stairs.

I hopped right after her.

"I'll kiss you right before I go to sleep," she said. But she pulled the covers over her head and quickly began to fake snore.

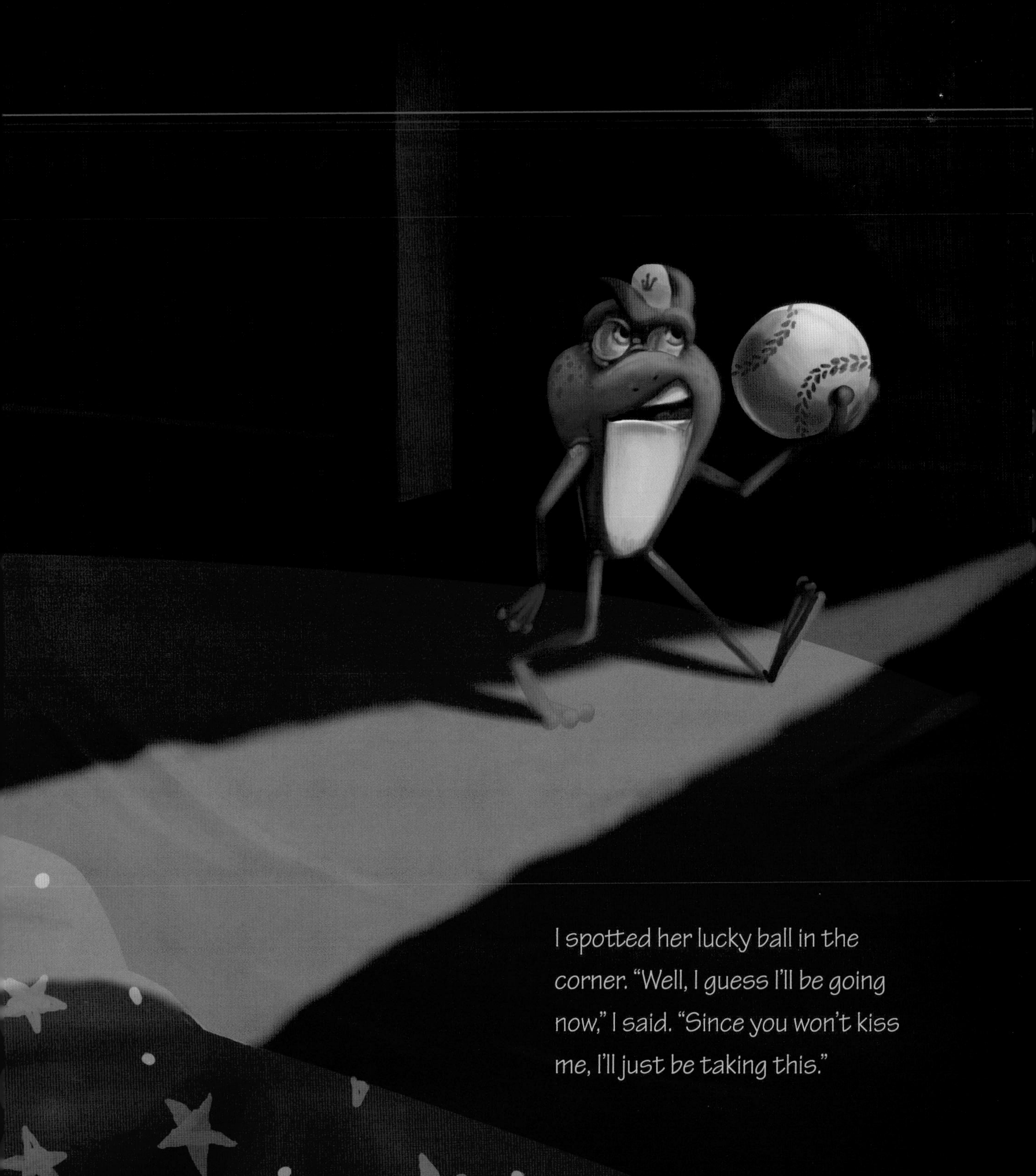

I spotted her lucky ball in the corner. "Well, I guess I'll be *going* now," I said. "Since you won't kiss me, I'll just be taking this."

The princess flung off the covers. "No! Wait! I'll do it!"

She picked me up and held me to her face.

She closed her eyes.

I closed my eyes.

Then—her lips touched mine. **"UGH!"** we both shrieked.

I felt myself being hurled into the air. And suddenly
I was stumbling around with two legs and two arms
that I didn't know what to do with.

"You're a prince!" she said.

"What an arm!" I said.

Did we fall in love, get married, and live happily ever after?

NO WAY. But my team got a great new starting pitcher!

THE
END

Think About It

THE STORY OF BEAUTY AND THE BEAST AS TOLD BY THE BEAST

Imagine living in a world in which fairies, witches, or other magical beings could appear at any moment. How would that affect your actions?

THE STORY OF SNOW WHITE AS TOLD BY THE DWARVES

Fairy tales have been around a long time and often have many different versions. What version of *Snow White and the Seven Dwarves* do you know best? How is it different from this one? How is it the same?

THE STORY OF RAPUNZEL AS TOLD BY DAME GOTHEL

Dame Gothel never says she loves Rapunzel in this story, but she does. How do we know this? How does Dame Gothel show Rapunzel that she loves her? What does Dame Gothel say that tells us she cares about this girl?

THE STORY OF SLEEPING BEAUTY AS TOLD BY THE GOOD AND BAD FAIRIES

Edna, the Bad Fairy, isn't really bad in this version of the story. She just makes a lot of mistakes. Describe her blunders, then list the steps she takes to correct them. What role does her sister, Stella, play in the story?

THE STORY OF THE FROG PRINCE AS TOLD BY THE FROG

If the princess told the story instead of the frog prince, how would her point of view differ? What details might she tell differently?

DON'T BREAK THE SPELL! THERE'S MORE ...

THE OTHER SIDE OF THE STORY: FAIRY TALES WITH A TWIST

CINDERELLA

JACK AND THE BEANSTALK

THE LITTLE MERMAID

THE THREE BEARS

LITTLE RED RIDING HOOD

AUTHORS AND ILLUSTRATORS

JESSICA GUNDERSON

Jessica Gunderson grew up in the small town of Washburn, North Dakota. She has a bachelor's degree from the University of North Dakota and an MFA in Creative Writing from Minnesota State University, Mankato. She has written more than 50 books for young readers. Her book *Ropes of Revolution* won the 2008 Moonbeam Award for best graphic novel. She currently lives in Madison, Wisconsin, with her husband and cat.

NANCY LOEWEN

Nancy Loewen has published more than 100 books for children. Recent awards include: 2013 Oppenheim Toy Portfolio Best Book Award (*Baby Wants Mama*); 2012 Minnesota Book Awards finalist (*The LAST Day of Kindergarten*); and 2010 AEP Distinguished Achievement Award (Writer's Toolbox series). She's also received awards from the American Library Association and the New York Public Library. Nancy lives in the Twin Cities and holds an MFA in Creative Writing from Hamline University, St. Paul. She likes to read, garden, cook, walk her dog, and collect weird figurines from thrift stores.

TRISHA SPEED SHASKAN

Trisha Speed Shaskan has written more than 40 books for children. She was a recipient of a 2012 Minnesota State Artist's Initiative Grant and won the 2009 McKnight Artist Fellowship for Writers, Loft Award in Children's Literature/Older Children. Trisha received her MFA in Creative Writing from Minnesota State University, Mankato. She works as a literacy coordinator for an after-school program and teaches youth writing classes at The Loft Literary Center. Trisha lives with her husband, children's book author and illustrator Stephen Shaskan, and their cat, Eartha, in Minneapolis.

DENIS ALONSO

Denis Alonso was born in São Paulo, Brazil. When he was a kid, drawing was his favorite thing to do. With the support of his parents, he was able to improve his skills to become an illustrator. He graduated with a degree in Design from Faculdade de Belas Artes de São Paulo and has worked with clients such as Discovery Kids, MTV Brasil, Montegrappa, Unilever, Santillana Group, Editora Abril, and many others. He lives with his wife and dog, Mr. Spock, in São Paulo. When he is not drawing, he likes to practice boxing or cook with his wife.

CRISTIAN BERNARDINI

Born in Buenos Aires, Argentina, in 1975, Cristian Bernardini is a graphic designer and a graduate of the University of Buenos Aires. Currently Cristian does design work and illustration for various studios and publishers, as well as developments in the field of animation for both TV media and media in general.

GERALD GUERLAIS

Born in Nantes, France, Gerald Guerlais grew up in nine cities, wearing as many different shoes as his shoeseller parents sold. He graduated in 1998 from the National School of Applied Art (Olivier de Serres) and honed his craft at a web design company, an event studio, a video-games studio, and several animation studios. Aside from his work as an illustrator, Gerald manages the French Comics Artists Association "Rendez-Vous" and co-leads (with Japanese artist Daisuke Tsutsumi) the artistic and charity project "Sketchtravel," a real sketchbook shared by 70 illustrators from all around the world.

AMIT TAYAL

Amit Tayal is an award-winning illustrator. Working for almost a decade, Amit has produced a wide range of illustration styles, using both digital and traditional methods. Amit has worked at various publications and animation studios. His work has appeared in educational, children's, and comic books around the world and has won multiple awards.

Special thanks to our adviser, Terry Flaherty, PhD, Professor of English, Minnesota State University, Mankato, for his expertise.

Editor: Jill Kalz
Designer: Lori Bye
Art Director: Nathan Gassman
Production Specialist: Kathy McColley
The illustrations in this book were created digitally.

Design elements: Shutterstock

Picture Window Books are published by Capstone,
1710 Roe Crest Drive, North Mankato, Minnesota 56003
www.capstonepub.com

Library of Congress Cataloging-in-Publication Data
Gunderson, Jessica.
Another other side of the story : fairy tales with a twist / by Jessica Gunderson, Nancy Loewen, and Trisha Speed Shaskan ; illustrated by Denis Alonso, Cristian Bernardini, Gerald Guerlais, Amit Tayal.
pages cm.—(Nonfiction picture books. the other side of the story.)
Summary: "Introduces the concept of point of view through retellings of five classic fairy tales - 'Beauty and the Beast,' 'Snow White,' 'Rapunzel,' 'Sleeping Beauty,' and 'The Frog Prince' - by the stories' supporting characters"—Provided by publisher.
ISBN 978-1-4795-5739-4 (paper over board)
1. Fairy tales—History and criticism. I. Title.
GR550.G86 2014
398.2—dc23 2013046717

Printed in China.
022015 008771